Ospreys in Danger

Pamela McDowell

Illustrations by Kasia Charko

ORCA BOOK PUBLISHERS

Library and Archives Canada Cataloguing in Publication
McDowell, Pamela, author
Ospreys in danger / Pamela McDowell ;
illustrated by Kasia Charko.
(Orca echoes)

Issued in print and electronic formats.
ISBN 978-1-4598-0283-4 (pbk.).—ISBN 978-1-4598-0284-1 (pdf).
ISBN 978-1-4598-0285-8 (epub)

1. Osprey—Juvenile fiction. I. Charko, Kasia, 1949–, illustrator
II. Title. III. Series: Orca echoes ·
PS8625.D785086 2014   jc813'.6   C2013-906851-1
c2013-906852-x

First published in the United States, 2014
Library of Congress Control Number: 2013955772

Summary: Cricket attempts to reunite baby ospreys with their parents after
an electrical pole catches fire and destroys their nest.

Orca Book Publishers gratefully acknowledges the support for its publishing programs
provided by the following agencies: the Government of Canada through the Canada
Book Fund and the Canada Council for the Arts, and the Province of British
Columbia through the BC Arts Council and the Book Publishing Tax Credit.

MIX
Paper from
responsible sources
FSC® C103214

*Orca Book Publishers is dedicated to preserving the environment and
has printed this book on Forest Stewardship Council® certified paper.*

Cover artwork and interior illustrations by Kasia Charko
Author photo by Mirror Image Photography

ORCA BOOK PUBLISHERS
www.orcabook.com

Printed and bound in Canada.

18 17 16 15 • 5 4 3 2

For Don, who introduced me to the wind, bears, and red rocks of Waterton many moons ago.

Chapter One

"I love the smell of Mondays." Cricket McKay tilted her nose up and closed her eyes. Her real name was Jenna, but everybody called her Cricket. It started back when she was five and collected hundreds of crickets on her grandpa's farm, hoping to start a cricket zoo. She eventually released the crickets, but the nickname stuck.

"You're crazy, Cricket. Mondays don't smell," said her best friend, Shilo.

Cricket opened her eyes. "*I'm* crazy?" She watched Shilo tiptoe along the top of the stone fence beside the sidewalk. The fence wasn't high, but it guarded the RCMP headquarters in the tiny village of Waterton. "You'd better get off of there before Constable Peticlaire sees you. And by the way, Mondays *do* smell…of popcorn!"

Shilo sniffed the air. "Mmm, you're right. Sabina always makes extra popcorn on Mondays."

Every Monday, a new movie started at the theater in the old Waterton Opera House. Since March, when both girls had turned nine, they had been allowed to walk to the theater together on Monday evenings.

A horn beeped. Shilo yelped and jumped off the fence. The girls turned to see a big white park-warden truck pull into the driveway at RCMP headquarters.

"What's your dad doing at the police station?" Shilo asked.

Cricket shrugged. "I dunno. The campgrounds are getting full. Maybe a bear broke into somebody's cooler."

Cricket's dad was a warden in Waterton Lakes National Park. He spent a lot of time sorting out disagreements between wildlife and tourists.

The girls waved to Warden McKay, then crossed the street to the theater. They lined up at the ticket window outside and then Cricket bought some licorice from Sabina at the snack counter.

Cricket and Shilo climbed the stairs to the first row of the balcony. Because the theater was in the opera house, it had scrunchy seats and no cup holders—but the balcony was cool.

The lights dimmed, and Cricket opened her licorice. In the middle of the third preview, the screen suddenly went black. The theater was completely dark.

"What's going on?" Shilo's voice was tense.

Orange emergency lights snapped on. The exit near the stage glowed. The girls looked at each other, their eyes wide. Nothing like this had ever happened before.

"Um, sorry, folks," Sabina's voice echoed through the theater. "We've completely lost power. There's no fire, no emergency, but please exit the building."

Cricket tucked the licorice into her pocket, and the girls felt their way down the stairs. Sabina directed everyone out onto the sidewalk.

"The lights are off everywhere," Cricket said. She pointed down the street, where people huddled outside dark restaurants and stores.

"Great," Shilo said. She squished closer to Cricket. She was a daredevil and a tomboy, but Shilo really didn't like the dark.

"Hey, here's my dad," Cricket said. The big park-warden truck stopped in front of the opera house. Its orange warning lights flashed, lighting up the street and people's faces.

Warden McKay lowered the truck window. "Do you girls want a ride?"

"You bet!" Shilo said.

The girls climbed in and did up their seat belts.

"The power's out all over the village," said Warden McKay. "I've got reports of a problem near the front gate. Would you girls like to come on an adventure with me?"

Cricket smiled. "Sure thing, Dad."

Warden McKay drove through the darkened village. Windows that should have sparkled with light were flat and dark.

"This is kind of creepy," Shilo said.

Warden McKay scanned the tree line as he drove.

"What are you looking for, Dad?"

"Something must have knocked the power line down. Can you keep a lookout?"

"Sure." It was hard to see the power lines in the dark.

"Do you smell smoke?" Shilo asked.

Cricket inhaled deeply. "Like campfire smoke?"

"Sort of."

Warden McKay slowed down.

"Nope. That's no campfire," he said. On the edge of Beaver Pond, an electrical pole was on fire. Flames shot high into the black sky.

"That's the pole the osprey nest was on!" Cricket exclaimed.

Every April, three pairs of ospreys arrived in Waterton after a long migration from South America. One pair kept coming back to its nest on the power pole at the park entrance. Each spring, it raised a new family of baby ospreys.

Warden McKay parked the truck and checked that the power lines were still attached to the pole. He handed the girls two large flashlights. "I'm going to radio the fire department. You girls search for birds—but don't get too close to the pole."

The girls stepped carefully through the tall grass that bordered the pond. They didn't know if they were looking for eggs, chicks or an injured adult osprey.

The howl of a siren grew louder. The Cardston Fire Department was on its way.

Chapter Two

In minutes, the flashing red lights of the Cardston Fire Department trucks lit up the night. The trucks pulled onto the grass and turned off their sirens. The engines rumbled like the deep growl of a bear.

Cricket and Shilo ran over to the trucks, where Warden McKay was talking with the firemen.

"I don't know if there is any power in those lines," Cricket's dad said, pointing to the overhead lines that came into the park.

The fire chief frowned. "It's too dangerous to spray water on them until we know if they have power.

The fire might burn itself out, but embers could spark a new fire in the grass." He directed his crew to carry fire extinguishers out near the pole.

Warden McKay turned to the girls. "Did you find anything out there, girls?"

Cricket and Shilo shook their heads.

"Search quickly. I'm going to help drag the hoses out there. If we need to blast the pole with water, you can't be in the way." He reached into his truck for a heavy canvas bag. "When you find them, put the chicks in here so you don't get scratched or bitten."

The girls ran back through the grass. They needed to find the osprey babies fast, before the chance for rescue was gone.

"Do you see anything?" Cricket called to Shilo.

"Not yet—but hey! Watch out!" Shilo covered her head and ducked as something swooped out of the darkness. It was an adult osprey! A high-pitched whistle screamed through the air. The osprey

swooped at Cricket. Its talons were stretched out in front of it, aimed at her head.

"Yikes!" Cricket covered her head with her arms and crouched low in the grass.

The osprey circled. It whistled a few more times, then flew off into the darkness.

"Wow! That freaked me out!" Shilo's eyes were huge.

"That osprey was defending something. We must be close," Cricket said.

Cricket spotted something in the stiff brown grass. It was fluffy and tan-colored and only about the size of her fist. The fluffball opened its black beak and squawked.

"Found one!"

"Really? Is it okay?"

"I think so." The chick tried to peck Cricket's hand as she nudged it into the open bag.

"Hey! Here's two more," Shilo said.

Cricket rolled them into the canvas bag. "They seem stunned," she said. "I hope they're okay."

Warden McKay joined the girls. "Did you find any birds?" he asked.

"Yup. We found three chicks." Cricket opened the bag for her dad to have a peek.

"Good work, girls. They still have their fluff, so they must be really young, maybe only six days old."

"Wow," Shilo said. "Do you think there are any more?"

Warden McKay shook his head. "An osprey clutch is almost always three eggs. Sometimes two, but I've never seen four. Let's get out of the way now and let the firemen take care of this mess."

They walked back to the truck and climbed in. Cricket settled the canvas bag onto her lap.

"What's going to happen to the chicks now, Dad?"

"I don't know, Cricket. If we had left them on the ground, they almost certainly would have died or been eaten. Osprey chicks rarely survive away from their parents."

The girls looked at each other. Shilo nudged Cricket with her knee.

"We can look after them, Dad. Shilo and I will take care of them until you can get them back with their parents."

Warden McKay shook his head. "This isn't like taking home a kitten or a puppy—or even a bucket of crickets. Ospreys are wild animals, and they will have to go back to the wild as soon as possible. Do you understand that?"

The girls nodded. "We can do it," they said.

Chapter Three

Cricket found a large cardboard box in her garage and carefully set the canvas bag inside it. The three chicks escaped the bag. They hopped and bobbed around the box. One chick straightened his legs and stretched his neck to see over the side. All three of them were covered with tan-colored down that didn't look like feathers at all. Their wings flopped. Their beaks looked razor sharp. When they weren't squawking loudly, the chicks stretched their mouths wide open.

"They sure look hungry," Shilo said.

"What do baby ospreys eat?" Cricket asked.

"I dunno. Can we call your dad?"

Cricket shook her head. "He's busy with the firemen. But I bet Mom will help. Let's go see what's in the fridge."

Mrs. McKay helped them search for anything that might look tasty to a baby osprey. Cricket carried a strange picnic of raw chicken and broccoli to the garage.

"What do you want to try first?" Cricket asked.

"I think they'll like the chicken best. It's meat and it's raw—perfect for a wild animal," Shilo said. She dangled the raw chicken in front of the chicks.

All three ospreys pecked at the meat, then started squawking again. When she dropped the piece of broccoli into the box, the chicks hopped backward, as if she had thrown a snake in with them.

Shilo laughed. "They like vegetables as much as I do."

Cricket shook her head. "Maybe they're just not hungry enough."

"What are you going to do with them? Are you going to leave them in the garage?"

Cricket looked around. The garage was small and dark and smelled like car exhaust. "Nope. Got any other ideas?"

"They would probably like to be up high," Shilo said. "What about my tree house?"

Cricket nodded slowly. Shilo's tree house was their favorite hideout.

"Being outside would be good," Cricket said. "But the chicks wouldn't have anyone to protect them.

They'd probably attract all kinds of other animals with so much squawking."

"Right. So maybe not outside," Shilo said.

"I guess in my bedroom, right by the window, would work."

"Sure. They'll be safe there."

Shilo led the way into the house as Cricket carried the box in both arms. They climbed the stairs to Cricket's bedroom on the top floor. Cricket placed the box on her dresser, right in front of the window, and Shilo raised the blinds. The moon was bright and full.

"There you go. That's a better view than the garage and safer than the tree house," Shilo said.

The chicks immediately began to squawk.

"Does that mean they like it?" Shilo asked.

Cricket shrugged and rolled her eyes. It was going to be a long, noisy night.

Chapter Four

"Hey, Cricket, are you in here?" Cricket's older brother raised his voice over the chicks' squawking.

Cricket groaned and pulled the pillow off her head. "Tyler? Is it morning yet?"

The osprey chicks fell silent, as though they were listening to the conversation.

"Barely. How can you sleep with all that noise?"

"I can't," Cricket said. She rubbed her eyes and sat up. "The chicks must be hungry, but they wouldn't eat anything we gave them last night."

Shilo's red ballcap poked through the doorway. "I've brought a couple of things they might like." She unwrapped a napkin in her hand.

Cricket raised her eyebrows. "Scrambled eggs and bacon?"

Tyler sniffed the bits of food. "They smell funny."

"The power's still out, so my mom used the barbecue to cook." Shilo nibbled a tidbit of bacon. "Tastes okay though. Want to try some?"

Tyler raised his hands and backed toward the doorway. "No, thanks! I'm going to go do some research and find out what those birds really eat—and I'm sure it's not scrambled eggs!"

Shilo shrugged and turned to Cricket. "Where's he going to do research? There's no Internet with the power out."

Tyler's voice echoed from down the hall, "I'll have to do it the old-fashioned way—with books!"

Cricket rolled her eyes, and both girls laughed.

Shilo watched the osprey chicks while Cricket got dressed. They didn't move when she dropped the bits of bacon and scrambled eggs beside them.

"They must be hungry," Shilo said. "Ospreys are like eagles, right? And eagles eat mice and dead stuff, don't they?"

Just then there was a knock on the bedroom door.

"Come in!" Cricket called.

Tyler walked in, carrying an open encyclopedia. "Boy, they don't look anything like a full-grown osprey," he said. "Are you sure you got the right birds?"

The girls turned to look at the picture he had found. The adult osprey had a sleek white head and dark wings, very different from the fluffy chicks in the cardboard box.

"Is that the bird that swooped at us last night?" Shilo asked.

"I think so," Cricket said. "Does it tell you what they eat?"

"Yup. They only eat fish. It says here they don't fly more than six miles from their nest to find food."

"So these ospreys must have been eating fish from the pond or Waterton Lakes," Shilo said.

"And they need about six pounds of food a day," Tyler read.

"Each?" the girls said at the same time.

Tyler looked up. "I don't know. But we better go fishing before they starve. Good thing school is canceled."

✳ ✳ ✳

Beaver Pond was a long bike ride from Cricket's house. When they finally arrived, the girls flopped onto the grass to catch their breath. Tyler propped his bike against a picnic table.

"Hey, cool, the guys from the power company are here," he said. The big green FortisAlberta truck was parked near the charred power pole. The bucket of the truck lifted one man up to work on the power lines while another man watched from the ground.

"I'm going to see if they know how the fire started," Tyler said and took off through the grass.

Shilo snapped the fishing rods together and straightened the lines.

"Ew, what's that?" Cricket pointed to a lump of worms in the tackle box.

Shilo shook a worm free of the lump and speared it with the hook. She laughed at the disgusted look on Cricket's face. "It's plastic, silly. Here, put one on your hook."

The plastic worm felt wiggly and squishy, like a real worm. Cricket threaded it onto her hook. Then the girls cast their lines. Shilo's reel zinged as her hook soared through the air and then plunked into the water. Cricket forgot to release her reel before casting and nearly snagged Shilo's hair.

"Oops, sorry!"

Shilo reached over and flicked a switch on Cricket's reel. "Now try," she said.

Cricket's next cast launched the hook. "Yay!" she cheered.

A gray jay swooped down onto a perch beside her. He tilted his head and winked at her, begging for a handout.

"Catch anything yet?" Tyler asked when he joined them at the edge of the pond.

Cricket shook her head.

"Did the crew tell you how the fire started?" Shilo asked.

"It was the ospreys' fault, all right. They built the nest too big, and sticks hung over the sides. One of those sticks probably touched both power lines and started the fire," Tyler explained as he cast his line far out into the pond.

The gray jay suddenly took off. A high-pitched whistle cut through the quiet, and the kids turned to see the osprey diving at the Fortis crew. The man in the bucket quickly pulled a metal shield over his head, protecting himself from the bird's vicious talons. "Wow, she really doesn't like them messing with her nest!" Shilo said.

"There's almost nothing left of it," Cricket said. "Tyler, did the crew say how they are going to rebuild the nest?"

Tyler shook his head. "They're working on getting the power hooked up again for the village."

"But the osprey chicks need their nest back right away," Cricket said.

"Hey, look." Tyler pointed out over the pond.

The osprey circled high above the water. She folded her wings close to her body and dove straight down. At the very last second, she lifted her head and plunged feet first into the pond, disappearing in the splash. Then she rose, her wings flapping heavily. She struggled as though something was pulling her back into the water.

"She's got a fish!" Tyler yelled.

"Cool!"

"Wow! Look how big it is!" Cricket said. She felt a tug on her fishing line. "Hey, I've got one too!"

Chapter Five

The osprey chicks were hungry. Their squawks echoed all the way down the hall from Cricket's bedroom.

Shilo grabbed a fish from Cricket's backpack and held it over the box. The chicks stopped squawking immediately. When Shilo dropped the fish into the box, the chicks pecked at it once or twice, then squawked again.

"Why aren't they eating it?" Shilo asked.

Cricket frowned. "Maybe they can't," she said. "Maybe the mother osprey drops the food into their mouths, just like robins do."

"So we need to cut it up."

Cricket ran downstairs. When she returned with a knife and tongs, she cut the fish into tiny pieces. Shilo held a chunk over the chicks, but they didn't open their beaks. One chick reached out and grabbed the piece of fish, swallowing it whole.

Tyler walked into Cricket's bedroom. "Do they like it?"

"They love it! I hope we have enough," Shilo said.

"But what if they start to think you're their mom?" Tyler asked. "If they get used to people, they won't want to go back to their nest."

Shilo stepped back so the chicks couldn't see her. "Maybe we could hide behind something when we feed them," she suggested.

"I have an idea," Tyler said, dashing to his room. He returned with a giant poster board that he propped up on the dresser.

The cardboard completely blocked the chicks from view. Within minutes, they were silent.

"You can thank me later," Tyler said as he headed out the door.

The girls waited for a few minutes, listening. "Do you think they're okay?" Shilo asked.

They peeked around the cardboard. The three ospreys were piled in a corner with their heads resting on each other. Their eyes—and beaks—were closed.

"Finally!" Cricket whispered. "I was beginning to think they never slept."

The girls tiptoed toward the door. Suddenly, the overhead light snapped on. The radio on Cricket's desk burst to life.

"Ahh!" Cricket dove for the radio and smacked the Snooze button. Shilo swiped at the light switch.

"Cricket! Tyler! The power's back on!" Mrs. McKay called from the bottom of the stairs.

"What are you girls doing? I smell something fishy here. Like, really fishy," she said, covering her nose.

"Shh, Mom. The ospreys are sleeping," Cricket whispered.

Mrs. McKay lowered her voice. "You need to make a plan, Cricket. The whole village has power, so you'll be going to school in the morning and I'll be working at the post office."

Cricket and Shilo looked at each other in dismay.

"We're going to need a lot more than two fish, Cricket."

❋ ❋ ❋

The girls were used to the wind in Waterton. It blew almost constantly. That afternoon the wind pushed the girls all the way up the hill along the pathway out of the village. They parked their bikes beside the picnic table and dropped their backpacks.

"Hey, look, the Fortis crew is still here," Shilo said. The green service truck was parked beside the power pole.

Cricket frowned. "What did they do with the nest? It's completely gone!"

"Do you think they forgot the chicks need to come back?"

"I dunno, but we better find out."

The foreman waved as the girls approached. "Hello, Jenna," he said. "Are you looking for your dad? He just left. Something about a porcupine in someone's tent, I think."

"Hi, Mr. Sprague," Cricket said. "This is my friend Shilo. She helped me rescue the osprey chicks last night."

Mr. Sprague nodded to Shilo. "That was good work, girls. How are the birds doing?"

"They're good, but they sure eat a lot of fish," Cricket said. At the top of the power pole a Fortis worker was attaching a big triangular piece of fiberglass to the crossbar.

"What is that?" Cricket asked.

"That's a new anti-nesting device," Mr. Sprague explained. "It covers the top of the power pole so birds can't land."

"But where are the birds going to build their nest?" Shilo asked. "This pole has been their home for years."

Mr. Sprague took off his hard hat and wiped his forehead with his sleeve. "I'm sorry, girls, but we can't let the ospreys rebuild their nest on the pole. It's just too dangerous. If you can come up with another idea, I'd be glad to hear it."

Shilo and Cricket looked at each other. How were they going to reunite the chicks with their parents if they didn't have a nest?

Chapter Six

"Hey, Cricket. Everything okay in the bird nursery this morning?" Shilo swung her backpack over her shoulder and joined Cricket on the sidewalk.

"Yup. The chicks fell asleep as soon as I fed them. I left some chunks of fish in the box, so they should be okay until school gets out."

The girls headed down the block toward Waterton Elementary School. Tyler caught up to them.

"We need to come up with a way to rebuild that nest," Shilo said. "Why do you think they built it on the power pole anyway?"

Cricket shrugged. "The trees might be too far away from the pond."

"The power pole is really secure too," Tyler added.

The girls stared at him. "Secure from what?" Cricket asked.

"Oh, snakes and raccoons and stuff. Predators like that might eat the eggs before they hatch. And the pole is really sturdy—I mean, it was before it caught on fire."

"So a pole is a good thing for a nest," Shilo said.

Tyler nodded. "Sure. Except for the power lines attached to it."

"What if the nest was up higher, maybe on a platform above the lines?" Cricket suggested.

"Yeah, or lower, so sticks wouldn't hang over and start a fire," Shilo said.

"Or even on a separate pole." Cricket was getting excited by their ideas, but just then the bell rang, and they had to run to class.

At recess, Tyler and Will, his best friend in grade six, had something to show the girls. The boys were grinning, and Tyler held something behind his back.

"We're building stuff in Science—" Tyler began.

"Mr. Tanaka wanted us to build a bridge," Will interrupted.

"Well, we built a nesting platform for the ospreys instead," Tyler finished. He held out a model built of popsicle sticks. A flat platform perched on top of a popsicle-stick pole. A ring of twigs was glued to the top.

"That's awesome, you guys!" Cricket turned the model in her hands and examined it closely. "It's as sturdy as the power pole but without the lines attached."

"We can nail some branches down to start the nest, so it won't blow off," Will said.

Cricket nodded. "Yeah, good idea."

Other students grew curious about what they were building—and why.

"Who's going to build the real platform?"

"It's going to cost a lot of money."

"And take a lot of machinery. That's a big pole."

They're right, Cricket thought. *We're going to need some help—and fast.*

"Why don't we write a letter to the Fortis crew?" Shilo said. "They have the equipment we would need. And the foreman, Mr. Sprague, said he wanted to hear our ideas."

"Yeah! We could all write letters!" The girls' classmates nodded to each other.

It looks great, Cricket thought. *But will the Fortis crew think so? Even more important—will the ospreys think so?*

Chapter Seven

On Friday, Shilo helped Cricket feed the chicks before school.

"They've grown so much, I think they're going to jump right out of the box," Shilo said.

"We have to get them back to their parents soon, but Mr. Sprague hasn't said anything about our idea," Cricket said.

The boys had presented their model to the crew foreman the day before, and the girls had given him seventeen letters from all the grade-three students at Waterton Elementary School.

"I guess we keep feeding them." Shilo picked up the last piece of fish with her tongs. "But you're going to need a lot more fish tonight. I've got track practice after school, so maybe Tyler can help."

"Maybe." Cricket felt a worried knot grow in her stomach.

✳ ✳ ✳

The boys had stayed late after school to finish their science project for Mr. Tanaka, and Shilo was at track practice. Cricket's mom was working at the post office, and her dad was fixing a fence up at Red Rock Canyon. Cricket was on her own.

She made a snack, packed up Tyler's fishing gear and headed to the pond. *Maybe I can talk to Mr. Sprague some more,* she thought. *Maybe the crew has already started building the platform!*

Cricket pedaled faster, eager to get to the pond.

But as she pulled up to the picnic table, she was alone. No Mr. Sprague. No crew. No FortisAlberta trucks. Cricket scanned the treetops—no osprey either.

It took a couple of tries before her hook landed out in the pond. Her first cast hooked the tree behind her. Her second cast snagged the reeds at the edge of the pond. Finally, her third cast sailed far out over the water, where it landed with a plunk.

"Yay!" Cricket tugged and reeled in the line. Nothing. Not even a nibble.

The hook was bare. The plastic worm had fallen off or been stolen by a sneaky fish. She reloaded the hook and cast again. And again. After seven tries, she still had not caught a fish.

Cricket sat on the picnic bench and hung her head. *No fish, no ospreys, no crew—no friends.*

Wink—wink? The same gray jay from before perched on the end of the table. He tilted his head and blinked. *Wink—wink?*

"Okay, maybe one friend." Cricket wiped her cheeks. "But I have to go, buddy. I have to get home before dinner."

Several trucks pulling fishing boats passed her on the road. At the main dock in the village, men worked at the washstand, cleaning their catches. Cricket watched them swipe large pieces of fish off the stand into buckets below.

Cricket's heart jumped. *That's not garbage*, she thought. *I know somebody who'll eat that!*

The fishermen were surprised but happily gave Cricket the scraps of fish. She held her breath and scooped the biggest pieces from the buckets. There was enough to fill both of her plastic bags!

When Cricket got home, she could hear the chicks squawking in her room. She opened the door and froze. The floor was a mess. Brown fluff and osprey poop were everywhere!

Cricket closed the door. Two of the chicks were under her bed. The third was still in the box.

"Tyler!" Cricket yelled. "Come quick!"

Tyler flung open the door. He looked at the mess

and quickly closed the door behind himself. "They got out, didn't they?"

"Help me get them out from under the bed," Cricket said. She grabbed a butterfly net from her closet and crouched down.

"Wow, they've really changed," Tyler said as he nudged the chicks toward Cricket's net.

The ospreys had lost their brown fluff and were now covered with black, woolly feathers. Their gray-blue legs seemed stronger as they hopped out of Tyler's reach. Their beaks looked as sharp as ever.

"They're starting to look more like birds," Tyler said.

"Yeah," Cricket said. "I just hope we don't have to teach them how to fly."

Chapter Eight

"Where's your dad going, Cricket?" Shilo asked. It was Saturday afternoon, and the kids were biking up the long hill. Warden McKay drove past them, heading in the same direction. He flashed the orange strobes at them and waved.

Cricket pedaled faster. They rounded the last corner, then pulled on their brakes in surprise.

Three FortisAlberta trucks had driven through the grass to the far side of the pond. Two of the trucks had their buckets extended to the top of a new pole, where the crew was attaching a large platform.

Cricket, Shilo and Tyler broke into cheers.

"They did it! They built it just like our model!" Tyler said.

The kids leaned their bikes against the picnic table, dropped their backpacks and helmets and raced over to Warden McKay.

"Hey, kids, you're just in time," he said. "The crew wants to secure some branches to the platform to get the ospreys started on a nest. Can you gather deadfall for the crew?"

"You bet!" Tyler and Shilo took off into the trees and searched the ground for fallen branches.

Cricket scanned the treetops for the ospreys. She hadn't seen the pair at all yesterday while she was fishing. *What if they've given up? What if they've abandoned the chicks and started a new nest somewhere else?*

Warden McKay put an arm around her shoulders. "They'll come back, Cricket, don't you worry."

As the Fortis crew lowered the buckets to load the branches, they heard loud honking. A Canada goose swooped down and landed in the unfinished nest. He honked and opened his wings wide.

"He's claiming the nest!" Tyler cried. "Canada geese steal osprey nests all the time!"

The kids turned to Warden McKay. "We have to do something, Dad," Cricket pleaded. "We can't let all this hard work be stolen by a lazy goose."

Warden McKay nodded. The crew rose up in the buckets. The goose hissed and opened his wings wide. The men waved their arms and shouted until the goose took off.

"Whew, that's a relief," Cricket said.

Warden McKay pointed to the trees behind her. "Now it's up to them."

Cricket turned to see both ospreys watching from the treetops behind her. They had come back!

"We need to go get the chicks, Dad," Cricket said.

Warden McKay nodded. "Let's take the truck."

They left Tyler to help the crew and headed back to the village. At the house, Warden McKay handed

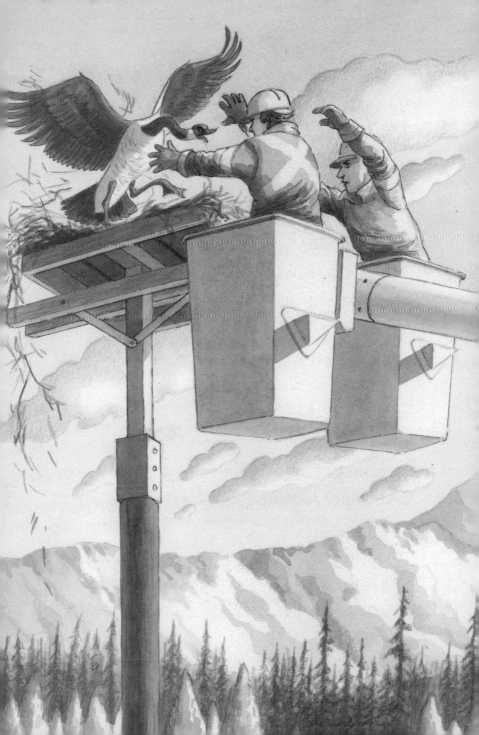

Cricket and Shilo a pair of heavy leather gloves each and a canvas bag.

"Dad, how do you know the ospreys won't reject the chicks?" Cricket asked. "If they smell like humans, maybe their parents won't want them anymore."

Both girls looked at Warden McKay, their eyes wide with worry.

"An animal like a fox or rabbit might reject a baby you had taken, but not ospreys," Warden McKay said. "In fact, sometimes older chicks beg for food at the wrong nest, and those adults will feed them."

"They don't even know their own babies?" Cricket asked.

"Well, I don't think they would feed a gosling, but they don't seem to mind feeding another osprey baby."

Cricket nodded. Maybe their plan *would* succeed.

* * *

After a few tries, the girls captured the chicks and climbed back into the truck. They headed back to the pond and bumped across the grass to where the Fortis crew stood on the ground, watching the sky.

"It looks like the nest is finished," Cricket said.

Tyler ran over as Warden McKay parked the truck. "The geese keep coming back. We chased them away twice!"

They jumped out of the truck and joined the crew.

"Who's going to release the birds?" Mr. Sprague asked.

Warden McKay hesitated.

"Can I do it, Dad? Please?" Cricket asked.

Warden McKay smiled and nodded.

Cricket's heart raced as Mr. Sprague handed her a hard hat. Her dad lifted her into the bucket with a Fortis crewman. He wore a hard hat and heavy leather gloves like Cricket. He also held the large metal shield to protect them from diving attacks. Cricket held on tightly as the bucket trembled and rocked, lifting them up. She spotted the adult ospreys in the treetops not far away. The bucket inched forward until it was right against the nest.

"Okay, you can release the birds, Cricket," the crewman said. "I'll keep a lookout."

She lifted the canvas bag into the nest and the three chicks tumbled out. They popped up as though surprised at their new surroundings.

"Goodbye, little chicks," Cricket said softly.

As the bucket lowered her to the ground, she heard the chicks squawk. But the adult ospreys didn't move from the treetops.

Warden McKay lifted Cricket from the bucket as they heard honking overhead. The Canada geese were back!

"Oh no!" Cricket cried.

They all watched as two geese circled the nest. Their honking was loud and threatening. The chicks' squawks changed to high-pitched whistles. The geese made another circle, flapping their huge wings and honking.

Then a dark shadow passed overhead. The adult ospreys swooped down on the geese. Their talons were extended like knives. Their beaks were open in anger.

Bodies collided. Wings flapped. Feathers flew.

It was over in a second. The Canada geese took off, honking angrily. The ospreys circled the new nesting pole. They seemed undecided.

Cricket held her breath. *Will they land? Will they recognize their babies?*

The chicks squawked again. One of the adults cocked its head, then swooped down to land on the edge of the nest.

"Yay!" The kids and crew cheered and high-fived. Cricket looked up and saw the second osprey heading back over the pond.

"Where's he going?"

Warden McKay looked where she was pointing. "I'll bet you he's gone to get something to feed those hungry babies."

"Thank goodness," Cricket said. "I was getting tired of all that fishing."

Warden McKay laughed. "Yes, you kids did a great job."

"And that nesting pole was an excellent idea," Mr. Sprague said. "If it works, Fortis may install more of them. That way, we can protect the birds *and* keep power running to our customers."

Cricket, Shilo and Tyler high-fived again. Mission accomplished!

Epilogue

In May 1977, a pair of ospreys really did cause the entire village of Waterton in Waterton Lakes National Park to lose power. Thirty years later, another nest atop a power pole near the park gate caught on fire and was doused by the Cardston Fire Department.

The power company, FortisAlberta, solved the problem by moving the power line and poles out of the wetland and erecting a new platform for the osprey nest. The company is focused on the safe delivery of electricity to 175 communities, but it is also concerned about protecting birds. Anti-perching spikes and fiberglass anti-nesting devices prevent birds from using power poles to build their homes. Colored flappers and curly bird diverters make power lines easier for birds to see and avoid.

Why spend so much money and time protecting ospreys? Ospreys feed at the top of the food chain on every continent except Antarctica. Ospreys do well in a region that is healthy. When an osprey population declines, we need to look for problems with the environment, like the contamination of water, erosion and loss of habitat. Responding to these problems benefits the ospreys and all the animals and people living in that region.

PAMELA MCDOWELL'S first career was in education, teaching junior high and high school. She began writing when she left teaching and has now written more than twenty nonfiction books for children. Pamela grew up in Alberta and enjoys writing about the diverse animals and habitats of her home province. *Ospreys in Danger* is her first work of fiction. Pamela lives in Calgary, Alberta, with her husband, two kids and an Australian shepherd.

For more information, visit www.pamelamcdowell.ca.